UP THE CREEK

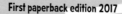

To the women in my life, Abbey and Sienna

First paperback edition 2017

Text and illustrations © 2013 Nicholas Oldland

Published in Canada and the U.S. by Kids Can Press Ltd.
25 Dockside Drive, Toronto, ON M5A 0B5

Kids Can Press is a Corus Entertainment Inc. company

www.kidscanpress.com

The artwork in this book was rendered in Photoshop.
The text is set in Animated Gothic and Handysans.

Edited by Yvette Ghione
Designed by Marie Bartholomew and Julia Naimska

Printed and bound in Shenzhen, China, in 6/2021 by C&C Offset

CM 13 0 9 8 7
CM PA 17 0 9 8 7 6 5

FSC
www.fsc.org
MIX
Paper from responsible sources
FSC® C008047

Library and Archives Canada Cataloguing in Publication

Oldland, Nicholas, 1972–, author, illustrator
Up the creek / Nicholas Oldland. — First paperback edition 2017.

(Life in the wild)
ISBN 978-1-894786-32-4 (bound)   ISBN 978-1-77138-798-9 (paperback)

I. Title. II. Series: Oldland, Nicholas, 1972– . Life in the wild.

PS8629.L46U6 2017   jC813'.6   C2016-905176-5

Kids Can Press gratefully acknowledges that the land on which our office is located is the traditional territory of many nations, including the Mississaugas of the Credit, the Anishnabeg, the Chippewa, the Haudenosaunee and the Wendat peoples, and is now home to many diverse First Nations, Inuit and Métis peoples.

We thank the Government of Ontario, through Ontario Creates; the Ontario Arts Council; the Canada Council for the Arts; and the Government of Canada for supporting our publishing activity.

UP THE CREEK

Nicholas Oldland

Kids Can Press

There once was a bear, a moose and a beaver who were
the best of friends, though they often disagreed.

One sunny day, the bear, the moose and the beaver decided to go canoeing.

The moose wanted to steer, but
so did the bear and the beaver.
They all sat in the stern.

With so much weight in the back of the canoe,
it tipped, and they ended up in the water.

So they played Eenie-Meenie-Minie-Moe, and it was decided that the moose would steer. They all settled back into the canoe and began to paddle.

The bear insisted on paddling portside, but the beaver and the moose also preferred the left. With everyone paddling on the same side, they traveled in circles.

Soon their arms grew tired,
so they began to switch sides. That's when
they finally started to travel in a straight line.
But just as they began to make progress, they
came to a stop at a beaver dam.

They all had different ideas as to how to get across.
The beaver wanted to push the canoe. But that didn't work.

The moose thought they should pull the canoe. That didn't work either.

Fortunately the bear figured it out. The only way across was to portage.

Back in the water, the bear, the moose and the beaver settled into a rhythm and started to really enjoy paddling along the river.

But it wasn't long before they began to argue. They argued so loudly that they didn't notice the current growing stronger or the quiet rumbling in the distance ...

Until it was too late!

The river had turned into wild white-water rapids.

Thrown sideways, underwater, through the air and everywhere, the bear, the moose and the beaver held on for their lives.

Exhausted, bruised and wet, the three friends landed on a rock in the middle of the rapids.

The moose wanted to burn the canoe to make a signal fire.

The bear wanted to throw the beaver to shore to get help.

The beaver figured swimming to shore would be safer.

They argued over whose plan was best well into the night.

The next morning, it dawned on the bear, the moose and the beaver that they would have to work together to make it home safely.

So they climbed back into their battered canoe,
took a deep breath and ran the rapids.

They twisted, leaped, crashed and blasted through the water.

The rapids were fierce, but
with the bear's powerful strokes,
the moose's steady hoof and
the beaver's clever commands,
they set a true, clear course.

At last, the bear, the moose and the beaver made it to shore.

After a much-needed nap, the bear, the moose and the beaver
worked together to repair their canoe and paddles ...

Catch some fish ...

And cook lunch.

Before they tucked into their meal, they all gave thanks for the wildest adventure they had ever had.

Rested and relaxed, the bear,
the moose and the beaver were ready to set out for home.

After taking a long look at the raging rapids, they decided
to walk. And who could disagree with that?

Dora's Big Dig

by Alison Inches
illustrated by Robert Roper

SCHOLASTIC INC.

New York Toronto London Auckland Sydney
Mexico City New Delhi Hong Kong Buenos Aires

Based on the TV series *Dora the Explorer*® as seen on Nick Jr.®

ISBN 0-439-83070-2

12 11 10 9 8 7 6 5 4 3 2 1   6 7 8 9 10 11/0

Printed in the U.S.A.

First Scholastic printing, April 2006

¡Hola! I'm Dora, and today I'm digging in the garden. Dig! Dig! Dig!

Wow! I uncovered a turquoise stone. Ooooh, maybe this is an ancient treasure!

I should take this stone to my *mami*. My *mami* is an archeologist. That means she digs for ancient treasure! She'll know what to do with an ancient treasure.

First I need to pick up my friend Boots.

Look, Boots! The stone has a jaguar's face carved into it, and the jaguar is wearing a crown.

Boots and I are going to need *your* help to get to the pyramid to see my *mami*. Who do we ask for help when we don't know which way to go? Yeah, the Map! Say "Map!"

Map says that we have to go across Emerald Canyon. Then we have to climb down the Steep Steps, and that's how we'll get to my *mami*.

¡Vámonos! Let's go!

Do you see Emerald Canyon? There it is! But it's so deep! How are we going to get across? Do you see something we can use to zip over the canyon?
Yeah! We can use the zip cord!

Wheeeee!

We made it over Emerald Canyon!

Uh-oh! Do you see Swiper? I think that sneaky fox wants to swipe our turquoise stone. We have to stop him. Quick! Say "Swiper, no swiping!"

Thanks for helping us stop Swiper. Where do we go next? That's right—the Steep Steps!

Do you see the Steep Steps? There they are!

Wow, these steps are really steep! Let's hold on to the rail.

We have to climb down ten steps. Will you help us count?
¡Uno, dos, tres, cuatro, cinco, seis, siete, ocho, nueve, diez!

We made it down the Steep Steps! Good counting! And there's my *mami* at the pyramid.

Mami says the stone belongs at the Museum of Ancient Art. We can take it there right away. *¡Vámonos!* Let's go!

The museum director says we found an ancient treasure—
the missing piece from the stone jaguar's medallion!

We can put the stone back where it belongs.

We did it! We found and returned the stone. *¡Gracias!* Thanks for helping!